P9-CCY-548

Phoebe Gilman

Pirate Pearl

North Winds Press
A Division of Scholastic Canada Ltd.

Canadian Cataloguing in Publication Data

Gilman, Phoebe,
  Pirate Pearl

ISBN 0-590-12495-1

I. Title.

PS8563.I54P57 1998   jC813'.54   C98-930658-5
PZ7.G54Pi 1998

6 5 4 3 2 1   Printed and bound in Canada   8 9 /901234/0

For Jason

Captain Plunk and his crew were rough,
rascally pirates, but they weren't the ones
who sank the ship. Count Crumple and his
evil friends did that.

"Ho ho! The fools forgot their treasure," said
Captain Plunk, pointing to something bobbing up
and down on the ocean waves. He thought it was
a chest full of precious pearls.

He was wrong. It was a cradle full of Precious Pearl.

"Precious Pearl is a *baby?*" he roared. "Make her walk the plank!"

But Pearl wouldn't.
Actually, she couldn't.
She hadn't learned to walk yet.
Captain Plunk had no choice.

He had to wait.

By the time Pearl learned to walk, the pirates were used to having her around. They decided to keep her.

"She's a regular lucky charm," said Macaroone. "Ever since she came on board, princes seem to sail right into our laps."

Pearl laughed merrily and bounced up and down on the overflowing treasure chest. The jingle-jangle of the gold set Captain Plunk's feet a-tapping and he danced a little pirate jig.

Yo ho! A pirate prizes,
Watching how the treasure rises.
Yo ho! We terrorizes
Princes without warning!

Pearl grew up to be a proper pirate.

"She can swashbuckle with the best of 'em," said Macaroone, beaming with pride. Captain Plunk even forgave her the one embarrassing habit she had: She didn't like to bury her treasure. She gave it away. At least, she tried to give it away. Most people ran when they saw Pearl coming . . .

but not Prince Basil. He had never met anyone quite like her. As soon as she leapt onto the deck of his ship, he was smitten.

Quicker than you can say "shiver me timbers," Pearl's trusty cutlass slashed the ruby buttons from his purple satin vest and flipped the royal crown off the royal head.

"I'll take that," she said, flashing a wicked pirate grin. "Thank you very much."

"She's very polite, too. Isn't she, matey?" said Captain Plunk, in case the prince hadn't noticed.

"Hand over the rest of your treasure," Pearl ordered.

But Prince Basil wouldn't. Actually, he couldn't. He had no treasure. The ruby buttons were glass. The crown was tinsel.

"I went to sea to seek my fortune," he explained, pulling a piece of paper from his pocket.

Hear ye! Hear ye!
Precious Pearl has been
captured by pirates

The usual reward for a princess rescue
is hereby proclaimed

Count Crumple

Pearl moved a step closer and looked at the paper. Prince Basil looked at Pearl.

"Oh, horrors!" he said. "That's Precious Pearl's locket! What have you done with the baby princess?"

"This is *my* locket," said Pearl. "I was wearing it when my Papas fished me out of the sea."

Hear ye! Hear ye!
Precious Pearl has
captured by

"Can it be?" said Prince
Basil. "Yes. It must be. You,
Pirate Pearl, are the lost princess.
I must say, you've changed quite a bit."
"Egads!" cried Pearl. "If I am a princess, a royal
treasure awaits. What are we lollygagging around
here for? Where's my castle?"

Ten days later, the pirates dropped anchor
in a small bay. Count Crumple was not happy to
see them.

"How dare you sneak into my castle?!" he said.

21

"*Your* castle?"
said Pearl. "I think you mean
my castle. I am Princess Precious Pearl!"
"Impossible!" said Count Crumple.
"I am the princess, and here is my princess
locket to prove it! I was captured by pirates,
just like it says on this proclamation you signed."
"Ha!" laughed the Count. "Precious Pearl was never
captured by pirates. She lies at the bottom of the sea."

"There's only one way you could know that," said Pearl. "You must be the one who sank the ship."

"Blast it!" cried Count Crumple. "I've been bamboozled by a buccaneer! My scheme was foolproof. How did you escape?"

"Nothing to it," said Pearl. "The ship sank. The cradle didn't. Throw the scurvy skunk in the dungeon!"

The people in Pearl's kingdom cheered. Nobody liked Count Crumple very much. He was a mean and greedy ruler.

"Now we shall be married and live happily ever after," said Prince Basil.

"Married?" said Pearl.

"Yes, of course," said Prince Basil. "That is the usual reward for rescuing a princess. You marry her and rule the kingdom. Everyone knows that."

"That's ridiculous!" said Pearl. "I won't do it!"

"Blow me down," said Captain Plunk. "This explains why all those princes kept showing up."

"But what about my reward?" said Prince Basil.

"Perhaps he could join our crew?" said Macaroone.

"I can think of no greater reward than that," said Pearl. She tossed a bag of treasure to the prince. "You can start by helping me give away this."

Yo ho! We like surprises,
Giving treasure scandalizes.
We could do no otherwises –
We are fearless pirates!